The BIKER'S Kiss

ROYAL BASTARDS MC

20 19

CHARLESTON, WV

Glenna Maynard

The Biker's Kiss © 2019 Glenna Maynard

ISBN: 9798645719951

The Biker's Kiss

One kiss is all it takes to bring him to his knees and have him asking for forever.

Roane Connors doesn't do relationships. He's been burned before and isn't looking to repeat past mistakes. All he needs is a warm body in his bed for the night. Someone to ring in the new year with. Julie Wilson ticks all his boxes. She's back in town, hot, and single. When the clock strikes midnight one kiss ignites a spark this royal bastard's not ready for.

ROYAL BASTARDS CODE

PROTECT: The club and your brothers come before anything else and must be protected at all costs. **CLUB** is **FAMILY.**

RESPECT: Earn it & Give it. Respect club law. Respect the patch. Respect your brothers. Disrespect a member and there will be hell to pay.

HONOR: Being patched in is an honor, not a right. Your colors are sacred, not to be left alone, and **NEVER** let them touch the ground.

OL' LADIES: Never disrespect a member's or brother's Ol' Lady. **PERIOD.**

CHURCH is **MANDATORY.**

LOYALTY: Takes precedence overall, including well-being.

HONESTY: Never **LIE, CHEAT,** or **STEAL** from another member or the club.

TERRITORY: You are to respect your brother's property and follow their Chapter's club rules.

TRUST: Years to earn it...seconds to lose it.

NEVER RIDE OFF: Brothers do not abandon their family.

Dedication

To First Loves and First Kisses.

Acknowledgements

To my fellow Royal Bastard authors, thank you for breathing life into this series and characters and for bringing me along for one hell of an exciting ride. Especially my girls, Crimson Syn and Nikki Landis. None of this would be possible without you bringing us all together. Kristin Youngblood and Mikki Thomas thank you for helping spread the word and for all the hard work you ladies do.

To my girls—Nickie, Dawn, Liz, Morgan, Jordan, Tempi, Andi, and so many more thanks for all the support while I was writing this and cheering me on till the end. If I didn't list your name forgive me, I have so many wonderful people who support me and I could never list you all, but I don't appreciate you any less. And Nickie thanks for being a trooper and looking at my cover 500 times until it felt right.

To Tina, who is so amazing and always ready to lend an ear, you're so good to me. I appreciate you more than you know.

My readers, I just can't tell you how much your continued support means to me. Thanks for continuing to ride with me on these wild adventures.

To my family, you are always so supportive of me and my dreams I love you for forever and a day.

Chapter 1

"**I** know you're lying, Sam. Just tell me the truth. I saw the cryptic messages between you and whoever Amanda is. How long have you been cheating on me?"

His hand flies back and whips across my face so fast that I don't even process what's happening until my cheek stings. Heat rises up my back and my stomach drops as I hold a palm to my flaming cheek. He hit me. Sam actually fucking hit me. I'm stunned as tears slide down my face. This man I thought I loved stares at me with pure venom in his eyes.

"I told you never to touch my phone." He takes a step toward me and I take a step back.

"You hit me. You coward."

Sam grabs my upper arms and shakes me. "You're a stupid cunt, aren't you?"

I know it's a mistake the moment I do it, but I gather my spit and pucker my lips letting it fly right at his face. "I hate you," I seethe.

"Oh yeah. You fuckin' hate me so much but you beg to ride my dick like it's made of gold." He smacks me again. This time splitting my lip. "You do nothing for me. I'm not attracted to your fat ass. Maybe if you'd lose some weight, I'd want to fuck you."

Fight or flight grips me, and I know if I don't make a plan to leave him now I never will. He won't let me. Sam has a reputation to uphold. He's a prominent attorney and in his cop daddy's eyes he can do no wrong. But Sam has developed bad habits lately. Cocaine and heavy drinking. He's changed. I have too. "I'm sorry," I lie. The only thing I'm sorry about is the fact that I ever thought I could love him. That I ever let him touch me. "I didn't mean it, honey. I don't know what came over me."

His eyes narrow on me, searching my face. His jaw unclenches. He strokes my cheek, then my lips, wiping the drops of blood away. "Go clean yourself up. We have dinner plans with Dan Ritchie and his wife Mary."

"Okay." I nod and he leans in for a kiss. My stomach lurches and it takes all my self-control not to vomit on his two-thousand dollar shoes.

**

One week later

"You can't tell me you're just going to sit here by yourself and watch the ball drop. That's so depressing, Jules." Pam stands in front of the Tv blocking my view hands on the hips of her black leather pants. My sister is a total bad ass biker babe. Her old man, Link, short for Chain Link, belongs to a motorcycle club, Royal Bastards MC.

"I don't even know anyone here." My friends are back home celebrating in style with my ex. There was no way I was going to tag along and watch him make out with his new girlfriend who also happened to replace me in my circle of friends. Some friends they were. The moment I broke things off with Sam everyone turned their backs on me like I had an infectious disease. I spent a few nights in a hotel. No one offered me a place on their couch. It was him or me and he won. He's the asshole who put his hands on me and everyone acted like I was crazy for being upset. Everyone wanted to make excuses for him.

Saying he had too much to drink. That I shouldn't have smarted off to him about staying out late the night before when it was Christmas Eve and all I wanted was to spend the holiday together. I shouldn't have gone through his phone. They were right about going through his phone. I should have broken things off the moment I started keep tabs on him. I knew I couldn't trust him. He was deleting messages and keeping secrets.

Turned out he had been cheating on me for months and they all knew it. I should have known. It had been months since we had been together intimately. I confronted him and when he smacked me a switch flipped. No one had ever treated me like that. It was the last straw.

Pam had been begging me to come stay with her and Link, and I had some vacation time to cash in at work before the end of the year so here I am camped out on her couch hiding from my life. It was either use the time or lose it and I've missed my big sister. I haven't told her the truth about Sam. I told her we broke things off because neither of us were happy which is mostly true, but we still share the apartment. I spent the rest of the week sleeping in the guest room and avoiding him at all costs. I've been looking for a place but haven't found something I can easily afford on my own. I rent a stylist chair from a salon in the mall. I'm not exactly rolling in money as a color specialist. I wouldn't have been able to come visit Pam if she hadn't offered to pay for my gas.

"You know me. That's all that matters. The club's throwing a huge party. You've got to come." She pouts her dark red lips out making a sad face. "Please, Julie. It'll be fun. Promise."

Pam only calls me Julie when she's trying to mom me.

I roll my eyes. "Fine, but I don't exactly have anything to wear." I look down at my bleach stained yoga pants and Mickey Mouse t-shirt.

"Leave that to me."

"You swear you won't make me look like one of those what did you call them, club rabbits?"

Her head goes back as she laughs. "Oh, sweet sister, I have so much to teach you tonight."

"That sounds like a warning."

"Oh, it totally is. The guys are going to love you." I don't like the mischievous glint she has in her eye. Pam has always been a wild child party lover and what some might call loose. Well until she got with Link a few years back the loose part changed, but she still loves a good party.

Pam ushers me to her bedroom. "Sit."

I drop my bottom on the round seat of her vanity already feeling the pangs of regret. When we played dress up as kids, I swear she made me look like a clown on purpose. Who knows what she will do with me tonight.

"Plug this in." She hands me the plug end of her flat iron. Pam and I both have dark naturally curly hair. I never wear mine straight. "It's time to spice things up and take a walk on the dark side." My sister smirks at me through the reflection of the mirror.

"Oh god," I groan. "I'm going to look like a two-bit hooker, aren't I?"

"What's that supposed to mean? You saying I look cheap?"

"No. You look wicked cool, but I don't know the first thing about being a biker babe."

"You'll learn fast. But the guys will behave. I'll tell them you're off limits."

"Might as well hang a sign around her neck that says virgin." Link chuckles from the doorway of the bedroom.

"Oh, hush, you." Pam smacks at him with her hairbrush.

"Well hello to you too," he says on a grunt.

"Don't be a grump. You know I missed you, honey." She goes up on her tiptoes to kiss her husband.

Link is exactly the kind of man I pictured my sister running off with when we were growing up. He's tall and big with tattoos on his face that say, *'Yeah, I did time, what of it.'* He's bad ass and not the kind of guy you want to piss off. But if he likes you, he can be a big ol' teddy bear.

Link folds his arms over his chest. "You coming to the clubhouse you gotta know the rules."

My brow shoots up. "Rules?"

"Leave her alone," Pam tells him, running the brush through my hair then rubbing in some smoothing serum.

"Hey. I'm only looking out for her."

"Well, Jules is a big girl. She can take care of herself. Why don't you go get us some drinks?" She waves him off and he pushes away from the door.

"What's this rules business?"

"Nothing really. Just don't be starting trouble. Which I know you won't be. Look, things will be wild and loud. Use your imagination then think of it being ten times crazier."

"Uh huh. Very helpful."

"I know." Pam glides her flat iron through my hair and Link returns with shots of dark liquor.

I gladly take my shot and another. It burns down my throat and warms my belly. I'm going to need liquid courage for the night that awaits me. Of course, since Pam got with Link, I've been privy to some stories but hearing about something and experiencing it are two different things.

Pam claps her hands together. "Makeup, clothes, shoes, and then we can go." She gives Link a look before he dares to open his mouth and complain that we're taking too long to get ready. He does however glance at his watch and mutter under his breath before taking another shot and leaving the room.

"Shit. If you weren't my sister, I'd bang you myself." Pam laughs.

"You're sick. You know that?"

"I take my meds." She smirks. "See for yourself. I'm serious. I'm gonna have to break out my bat to keep the guys off you."

"Stop it." I turn to look at myself in the mirror and damn big sister didn't do me wrong. My hair is smooth and silky. Lips stained red and eyes done up dark and smoky.

"Told you. Now put this shirt on and these jeans. They might be a little tight on your ass but that's a good thing."

I shake my head. Pam has always been blunt and never one afraid to speak her mind. The woman has no filter. I leave my Mickey tee on and shimmy out of my yoga pants.

"Please tell me that you have better panties than that." Pam eyes my white cotton boycut bottoms.

"What's wrong with these?"

"Nothing if you're eighty. We want to get you laid. I have some with the tags still." I fold my arms over my chest as she goes to the closet and pulls out a Victoria's Secret bag. "Take your pick. Consider it a late Christmas gift."

"Gee thanks, Sissy. Pretty come fuck me panties."

"And the matching bra. No wonder you and Sam had shit sex if that's what you were wearing to bed."

"Oh, shut up."

"I'm just sayin'."

"You can just say all you want out in the hall. Can I have some privacy please?" Truth is

I don't want her to see the bruises on my back. When Sam found out I was coming to stay with Pam he snapped on me and it got physical. In his twisted mind I'm still his even though we haven't been a couple for a long time. Sure, physically I was there but emotionally I had been done for a long time. Longer than I realized until it was too late. The only reason he didn't do more damage was because the neighbors heard and threatened to call the police on him. Not that it would have done any good. His dad is on the force and he's an attorney. At the time I was happy he didn't strike my face. If Pam knew she'd send Link after him, and I don't want him getting into to trouble for assault on my behalf. Though I'd love to see Link beat the hell out of him.

"Pfft. You act like I didn't used to wipe your ass when you were little."

"Yeah, and I'm thirty now so get out."

"How's the landing strip? You all good down there."

"I swear if you offer to wax me, I'm staying in."

"I was only going to say I have some bikini hair remover in the bathroom. Excuse me for wanting to make sure your shit's all nice."

"I'm good and I do appreciate you. But most big sisters don't encourage their baby sister to go hookup with a random biker in pretty come fuck me panties."

"That's because most big sisters aren't as bad ass as me. Thank you very much." She takes a bow and closes the door behind her.

"Crazy ass," I mumble and settle on a yellow lacey thong and matching bra. My sister is a fucking nut, but I love her to pieces. I have missed her so much. Being here and

15

spending so much time with her has me wondering if maybe I don't need a bigger change besides ending things with Sam. There is nothing keeping me in Cleveland. I could move here if I could find a job. I do miss getting to see Pam all the time. I need a clean break. I need away from Sam for good. Maybe her and Link will let me stay in the spare bedroom until I can get on my feet. I hate to ask her, but I don't think they'd turn me away.

I pull the jeans up and she's right they are snug on my ass, but I like the way they look on me. I slip the top over my head, it's a black sweater that hangs off my shoulders. My bra straps show though it's not like a bunch of bikers will give a shit or even notice. I twist around in the mirror double checking none of the bruising on my back is visible. They look worse than they are. I've been popping over the counter pain relievers to alleviate the discomfort. I drove here with ice packs between my back and the seat of my car hoping to get the swelling down. It helped a lot.

I finish my look with the black silver studded heels she laid out for me.

"Is it safe to come in now? Link is getting antsy," Pam calls out.

"I'm ready."

"Thank fuck," Link grits. "Let's go."

I grab my purse and while they get their jackets on, I pop a couple more pain pills for my back.

Chapter 2
ROANE

I roll up to the clubhouse, known to most as The Devil's Playground. I came here tonight for two things. To get drunk and get laid. Hopefully Murder brought some new girls in. I'm tired of the same old busted up pussy all my brothers have had a go at. It's New Year's Eve. A night for new beginnings and forgetting old regrets. Like my bitch of an ex, Leah. Cheating cunt. She had me fooled until I came back early from a run and caught her in bed with the fuckin' neighbor. I gave her the house and said fuck it all. I simply wanted rid of her. That was three years ago.

I've sworn off relationships. I'll never be another woman's fool. I walk in and to my frustration it's the same shit different day. I nod to Grudge and make my way to the bar to grab a beer. I spy my buddy East sitting at the end looking like someone kicked his damn puppy.

"Hey, Roane," Daisy purrs from behind the bar. Her nipple is hanging out of the black leather bikini top she's wearing. I doubt she even knows or cares for the matter. She's a club bunny. I've tapped her ass a few times but tonight I'm not feeling that desperate yet.

"Gimme' a beer."

"Sure thing." She winks and when she bends over to grab my beer from the barrel of ice, she flashes me her bare ass from under her denim skirt. East doesn't bat an eye at the sight either. It's nothing we don't see daily around here. Her ass is no longer new or special.

"What's eating you, man?"

"Nothing. Just not feeling this scene tonight." I look over his shoulder at his flashing phone screen. Wylla Mae is calling him. She's the daughter of one of his ex-girlfriends. Seventeen and a real beauty queen. I've never said shit to East about it but we both know the girl is crushing hard on him. Fucked up thing about it is, I've seen them together and they have this spark. I've never felt that with anyone in my adult life but if anyone deserves that kind of happiness its East, but he's fucked. Wylla Mae is about twenty years too damn young for the poor bastard. He slides his finger over the screen, hitting ignore.

I shake my head and accept my longneck bottle from Daisy. "Not much longer that shit'd be legal," I tell him.

"Fuck off with that bullshit. You know I don't look her that way."

He can lie to himself all he wants, but I'm calling it now. The damn minute Wylla Mae is legal they'll be fucking.

"You need to grab you a whore and go fuck that temptation out of your system." His eyes cut to me in warning. "I'm just saying, man. Girl has it bad for you." And he's got it just as damn bad for her. He can deny it, but I see it. We all do.

"Last warning before I put your head through the fucking bar," he growls, and I know I need to leave the poor bastard alone. I watch as he goes behind the bar, grabs a bottle of Jack Daniels, and stumbles upstairs to his room alone.

I shoot Daisy a smirk. "You should go see if he needs a Coke to chase that with."

"That's not a bad idea, but I'm covering the bar till Pam and Link get here."

"Go on. I don't have shit else to do."

"Thanks, Ro."

"Fuck his brains out. He needs it."

"Will do." She gets a can of Coke from the cooler and hesitates by the end of the bar. "You know you could find a friend and join us."

"You know damn well East and me ain't into that shit."

"It's New Year's. The night is full of possibilities."

I snort. "Yeah. Sure." Fuck that mantra garbage. I move behind the bar as Daisy sashays up the stairs in search of East. The music is loud, and the liquor is flowing. My brothers seem to be having a great time. Even Prez and his Old Lady are dancing. Ruthie is a pure bitch, but she has a smile tonight. It's rare

23

to see the two of them looking all loved up with one another. It's none of my damn business though I know Murder isn't happily married despite the appearance he tries to maintain. I scan the bar hoping to see someone I can get lost in for a little while. All I need to ring in the new year is to get my dick wet.

The front door opens and in struts Link and his Old Lady, Pam. Disappointment floods me and I grab another longneck and pop the cap off. Guess I'll be spending my night beating one out.

"Aren't you a pretty bar bitch." Pam laughs. I snap my head up as she moves behind the bar. "I brought you a present. I think you remember my sister, Jules. Behave yourself," she warns. "Jules, you remember Roane."

Fuck me. I glance behind her and see the most stunning woman who resembles the girl I dated back in high school, but she's all grown up now. It's like a bolt of lightning shoots straight to my dick and zaps me when I look at her. "Where the hell you been hiding at?"

"Cleveland," Jules answers. Her lips quirk into this sexy as sin smile.

Damn. She's gotten hotter. Smoking hot. Out of ten she's a damn thirty. I can't help but check her out. Damn she's filled out nicely. She's got full hips, a luscious ass, and big tits to match. I think I've died and gone straight to heaven. "It's a real pleasure to see you again, sweetheart. Anything Pam says about me is a lie." I chuckle. It's been at least fifteen or more years since I've seen her. We dated briefly in high school until she moved up north with her grandparents.

Before she can reply Viking, Crawl, and Grudge are elbowing their way to the bar with the same thought as me. Fresh pussy. Assholes need to back up. I saw her first. They need to go find their own woman. Tonight Jules is going to be mine. Hell, I always considered her the one who got away. She was my first love. I feel like fate is fucking with me. Dangling temptation in front of me.

"Well hey there." Viking holds a hand out to her.

"Name's Crawl."

"Call me yours." Grudge winks at her.

"Easy, boys. My sister is off limits. You can look but don't touch. She's visiting and here to have a good time. Jules is a good girl."

"Oh my," Jules says, mock fanning herself. "I think it's a little hot in here." *I'll make her think hot in here.*

"How about a drink?" I step in front of Jules, cutting my brothers off, and blocking their view.

26

"A drink sounds good. What'd you say your name is?" She teases me, pretending she doesn't remember me.

"Like you could fuckin' forget me."

"Hmm...you seem familiar." Lips lifting in a devious smirk, her memorable green eyes meet mine. I gaze into them seeing those flecks of gold I always loved. The colors paired together is mesmerizing. I hear the guys cursing behind me as Pam tells them to order a drink or beat it.

"What's your poison?"

"Surprise me."

"Blowjob? Sex On The Beach?"

"Wishful thinking." Her pearly whites graze her bottom lip.

"Baby doll, if I wanted to proposition you, I'd do it a helluva a lot smoother than that."

"Oh. You got game?"

I nod and fix her a blowjob. "You used to love my game."

"That was a long time ago." Jules reaches for the shot.

"Nu uh. Hands free. It's called a blowjob for a reason," I tell her.

Her ivory cheeks flush. "All right." She leans forward, holding her hair back with both hands, capping her mouth around the brim of the glass.

"You trying to corrupt my baby sister?" Pam leans into me.

"Maybe she's doing the corrupting. She's the one that wanted me to sneak her under the bleachers all the time to make out."

"Sure." She snorts. "But do me favor and watch out for her tonight. I don't want anyone taking advantage. Show her a good time. She needs it."

"You can count on me." I'll show her a good time all right. I'll fuck her brains out. I'll fuck her into January no problem. I'll fuck her like I should have all those years ago.

Jules plops the empty shot glass on the bar and arches her brow at me. "Done."

"Almost. You left a little cream right here." I swipe the whipped cream off the corner of her mouth and lick my finger.

"You did not just do that. I could have cooties for all you know."

"Cooties?"

"Yeah, herpes or something."

"And do you have cooties?"

"Well no…"

"All right then. Cootie crisis avoided. Besides, if you had cooties, Jules, I think I'd have caught them a long time ago. If I recall correctly, we spent a lot of time under them bleachers behind the football field when you should have been at cheer practice."

"Roane, get over here," Viking yells at me.

"Excuse me a moment." I stomp over to the table where he's sitting with Grudge and Crawl smoking a blunt. "The fuck you want?" Cock blocking shitheads.

"You going to take her upstairs and fuck her or do I need to do it for you."

"Shut the fuck up."

The three of them bust out laughing. Assholes.

"You sure you know what to do with her?" Grudge starts in. "I can draw you a diagram."

"I'll hold your hand if you need me to," Crawl says and takes a hit. "I can show you how it's done. You know which is the right hole?"

I grab the joint from him and look around to see where my girl took off to before I kill someone.

Chapter 3

"Roane can't take his eyes off you," Pam whispers in my ear and slaps my ass. I let out a yelp winning me the attention of half the clubhouse.

"Ow. What was that for?"

"Nothing. Listen, if you want to hook up with someone here tonight. You can't go wrong with Roane. He's been burned in the past by his ex, so he's not looking for anything but some fun. I'm just saying and before you get all I'm not fucking anyone on me. Hear me out. You dated loser Sam and you said yourself the sex was awful. I'm here a lot and I hear things ya know and well let's just say the girls around here talk and Roane...the brother can lay it down. But I guess you already know that. Didn't he punch your V-card?"

"Stop it. I swear you were dropped on your head as a kid. No. If you must know I was still a virgin when we dated. And you did this on purpose. You knew he'd be here."

"You need to get back on the horse. Go for a ride." She cackles like the witch that she is. "Giddy up." She motions her hand over head like she's swinging a lasso.

"I hate you sometimes."

"You love me. You know I'm right, and you hate it when I am smarter than you. But I'm older and wiser. Listen to me. You guys had chemistry then, just imagine how explosive it will be now. You're both older and more experienced. I'm almost jealous of the amazing sex you're going to have tonight. Fuck. You are going to have so many O's."

"I've always fantasized about you being a real cowgirl," Link teases and goes in for a big sloppy kiss, interrupting our conversation. The tender moment makes me a little sad. Pam is crazy but she has a man who loves her deeply. I'm not sure I will ever find that all consuming passion. I want it, but even with Sam I was going through the motions. He was too. I don't know why were even together as long as we were. I think I was more in love with the idea of finding someone than actually being with him. Growing up our parents were always fighting. When Dad went jail and Mom took off, I moved in with our paternal grandparents and they were together over sixty years. I envied them. I've always wanted that kind of love for myself. But I don't think I'm ever going to find it.

I catch Roane eyeing me from across the room and flames lick up my neck. My sister is right though. I could have worse prospects. Roane is sexy. He has this look that you know he'd be a good lover. He's grown into a man, but to be fair we were only kids when we dated. He puts Sam to shame in the looks department. Tribal tattoos mark his tanned skin. He has this rough edge to him. Dark eyes and facial hair that you know would scratch the right spots. Big hands. I look to his boots. Large feet. Pam always told me that big feet and big hands on a man meant a big dick.

The thought of sex makes me nervous. With Sam it wasn't good, but it was comfortable. I knew him. I know Roane but fifteen years is a long time. People change.

I don't know if I can do that again. Put in so much effort to be disappointed. Sam didn't break my heart, but our split hurt. I've come to realize I broke my own heart by being in a relationship I knew wasn't going anywhere, but I have this empty feeling. I'm lonely. A one-night stand isn't the worst idea. Maybe Pam is right, and I need to put myself back out there again. I glance around the room. There's plenty of sexy men here. The scene isn't as vulgar as I imagined it to be. Sure, there's drinking, smoking, dancing, and half naked women all around, but these are simply good people having fun. If Sam could see me right now, he'd shit his pants. He's a suit and tie guy.

Roane is as anti-Sam as I can get. All the men here are though and there's a lot of them to choose from but there's something about Roane that makes me want to see if there could be something between us, even if it's for one night. I always thought he was going to be my first. He's sexy and dangerous. Everything I should stay away from and yet I find myself returning his gaze and smiling. The way he's looking at me, makes me feel wanted. It's been some time since anyone has awakened that inside me.

"Let's dance," my sister shouts in my ear and grabs my hand. She drags me out to the floor where there's an empty space. I close my eyes and let the music carry me away. Swaying my hips side to side I get lost in the song. I look to see where Pam is and find her in Link's arms. He's kissing down her neck and squeezing her ass. I continue to dance alone and shake my booty to *Cherry Pie* by *Warrant*.

A firm pair of hands land on my hips and a large body presses into me from behind. "Make an old man happy." I turn my head up to see Grudge I think is his name. He's old enough to be my dad but handsome none the less. I nod and keep dancing. He seems harmless enough. I bump my ass up against him figuring I may as well give him a thrill. I came here to have fun tonight. I dance through another song with him then excuse myself back to the bar where Pam is waiting with another drink for me.

I knock it back and when I finish Roane is grabbing me by my hand and leading me back to the floor where it's gotten a lot more crowded. *Closer* by *Nine Inch Nails* is playing. This song simply put oozes sex. The beat makes my body move in ways that should be reserved for behind closed doors. I can't help myself. I'm feeling good and Roane is hot. He holds me close, knee pressed between my thighs. I grind against him. The beat of the music drums through my veins, pulsing through my blood as it pumps faster. His hands are on me everywhere. Desire burns between us. I want him. There's a primal attraction that I can't explain screaming for me to take control and take this man to bed.

Roane is staring at my lips and I wonder if he's as good a kisser now as he was back then. His gaze is intense. I spin around and press my ass against his crotch and holy shit either he's got a gun in his pocket or he's really fucking hard. His hands are rubbing up and down my sides. Lips at my ear, the man's voice sounds lethal. Dark and gritty. He sings the lyrics that talk about wanting to fuck like an animal. The sensation of his facial hair scraping over my skin mixed with his words has warmth pooling between my thighs. I'm so damn turned on right now.

The music cuts off and the countdown to New Year's begins. He holds me still, an arm across my chest. His thick hardon pressing into my ass. Roane's lips move against my neck. God his lips feel good. I count from ten with him. On five he tilts my chin upward and at one his mouth claims mine, searing my soul. Tasting of liquor, his tongue dominates mine. Deep and wet. Hard and slow the man makes love to my mouth with his kiss. It's a kiss that makes time stand still. The kind of kiss that makes you forget who you are and where you've been. When he palms my breast, I return to Earth and pull away absolutely breathless. I've never been kissed so erotically in all my life. My knees feel as though they may give out any minute now. I could fuck him right here I'm so aroused.

Roane doesn't relent or give me any reprieve. Those big hands grab my face, and he comes in hot and fast kissing me again with so much fire I might combust. Tongue thrusting deep in my mouth, his hands are on me. The world around us melts away. Right now, I don't even know my own name. "Upstairs," the word comes out in a growl that vibrates down my spine as he squeezes my hip, fingers biting into my skin with possession.

"Okay," I whisper. I think in this moment I'd go anywhere with him if he'd kiss me like that again. He's a better kisser than I remember. I didn't think that was possible, but the man has skills.

Chapter 4

ROANE

Fuck me, my pulse thrums in my ears as I navigate through the crowd. "Happy New Year," rings out from different directions, but I don't stop to return the sentiment. My hand swallows Jules' as I lead her to the stairway. Feeling like I'm travelling the stairway to Heaven. Electricity shoots through my veins at her delicate touch. Her fingers hook through my belt loops and I keep her close. I feel like she never left. I was consumed by her then and now all I want is to have her. Claim her body and remind her how good we were together.

Viking pats me on the back giving me a smug look as we pass by him. I hear Jules gasp and look down. Wendi is on her knees, lips suctioning Crawl's dick. His fingers fisted in her hair, yanking hard, fucking the hell out of her mouth. This party tonight has been tame compared to others, but I sense a shift in the energy around us. Clothes are about to come off. Mine are too, but I want Jules all to myself.

"You shocked or turned on?" I question, curious to hear her answer.

"Both," she responds, honestly.

I make note for the future. Jules has some voyeur in her.

We pass by an open door. East is passed out naked on the bed and hugging a now empty bottle of Jack Daniels. Daisy and Lynn are fighting outside his door. Lynn is screaming at her for fucking her man. I don't know why Lynn keeps coming back when she knows East is never going to claim her as his Old Lady. Prez will kick both them bitches out if he sees that cat fighting shit, but it's not my problem. Only thing on my mind is getting Jules under me. The woman has me so damn tore up I am fumbling to unlock the damn door. I don't know what it is about her, but from the moment I laid eyes on her all I've thought about is getting her naked. It was always like that between us though. When we were together no one else existed.

I jerk her through the door once I get it open. I don't bother with the light. I immediately start removing her clothes. Lifting her shirt over her head, I pause long enough to look at her tits all pretty covered in yellow lace.

Mouth back on those sweet lips, I yank the zipper on her jeans and work on getting them off her between frantic and fevered kisses. She goes for my shirt and it gets caught around my head. I say fuck it and rip the damn thing off.

Laughter erupts in her throat and fuck me it's the sweetest sound, one I remember well. So damn sugary my damn teeth ache. I drop my jeans and she licks her lips seeing my big cock. I get a handful of her ass, fuck yeah, it's big and thick. I like that. I like it more than a lot. I squeeze both cheeks. Pulling her flush against me, the head of my cock sliding between her legs. Fuck. She's already wet. I slide my palms over her hips up under her waistline of her thong, pulling the material tight against her pussy. Lips fused with hers, I walk Jules backwards till we reach the bed.

I shove Jules down gently by her shoulder, moving onto the mattress with her. Rolling back to rest on my calves I stare down at this beautiful woman and send a silent thank you up to Lady Luck for smiling down on me and bringing my girl home to me. Spreading my hands over her torso, I rub up and down her sides, trailing my fingers down her thighs and spreading her legs. Moving my thumb over her pussy, I tease her there mercilessly, while sucking on her neck till her hips are flexing up and her lacey thong is fucking soaked through.

Fingers threaded in my hair she moans one word like it's her only prayer, "Please." The whimper that follows after travels straight to my dick, but I'm not going to fuck her just yet. I'm taking my time. Jerking the cups on her bra down, I capture a nipple with my mouth and suck while massaging the other and pinching with enough pressure to bring her pleasure.

Nails scratching down my back, her legs thrash on the sheets. I nip and suck my way down her abdomen till I reach that pretty little pussy. I can smell her arousal and fucking hell if she doesn't smell like mine. Like she belongs to me and only me. Like she always has. I don't know what to make of the emotion coming over me. The feeling that's been in the back of my mind since I saw her walk in the clubhouse looking like she was sent from Heaven just for me. The idea of it is ludicrous, but here I am ready to go down on her. Something I don't do for the women I fuck. Something I've not done since my divorce. I don't put my mouth where others have been, and I never fuck without a condom. Jules isn't some random fuck though. Not for me. She's always held a special place in my heart. I never thought I'd see her again, but here she is. Ready and willing to give it up. To make my fantasy come true.

I slide her thong down her thighs, over her knees, and she kicks the yellow lace free from her ankles. Parting her pussy lips, I bury two fingers inside her and French kiss her clit. I'm rewarded immediately with the erotic sound of her whimpers and pleas. Jules is so damn responsive to me, better than I remember. It'd be easy enough to slide my cock right in that tight, wet heat right now, but I want to test her limits. See how far I can take her to the edge. Her walls clench around me. My dirty girl rides my hand hard.

Removing my fingers, I shove them in her mouth, and she sucks them deep, tasting herself. I bet she'd suck dick like a damn champ the way she's licking my fingers. We never got that far back in the day. Fisting my cock, I beat it against her sweet cunt, rubbing the head over her clit. Her slender hand wraps around my shaft, and I grin at how eager she is to have me filling her up.

"You want this dick?"

"Fuck me, Roane." Her fingers stroke me.

"Not yet." I brush the head against her cunt, sliding through her juices back and forth.

The look she gives me is deadly. I tease at her slit pushing the tip in and drawing back out. Dropping back to my calves, I fist my cock again, stroking my shaft as she stares at me with hungry eyes. "Come suck it," I demand and like a good girl she crawls toward me.

Lips parted she gazes up at me as I tower over her on my knees. Darting her tongue out she licks the pearly bead of precum and moans, sucking me deeper in her mouth. Those thick lips stretch around me, her deep green eyes going big and round. Tongue flat against the underside of my length Jules takes me to the back of her throat.

I cup my hand under her chin and caress her cheek. "That's it, baby doll." I thrust in and out of her wet, hot mouth until I'm on the brink of coming.

Popping free of her lips, I lay her back down and settle between her thighs, spreading her legs wide. I'm going to remind her that she always should have been mine.

Chapter 5

Holy shit this is really happening. I'm on my back underneath a sexy as sin tattooed god of a biker as he guides his thick cock inside me. Roane's gaze is on me the whole time, gauging my reaction as he sinks deeper in. I feel my body burning and stretching to accept his size. His dick is fucking huge. Biggest I've ever been with. He's got an impressive cock. I only touched it once when we dated. I was terrified of it then and even more so now, but I want this. I want him.

Hot and greedy his mouth devours mine. One hand on my throat and the other gripping my hip as he stuffs me with his girth and length.

The man has me pinned down and unable to move. Releasing my mouth, he draws back and slams back in, repeating the motion hard and fast. My tits bounce with the movement as he hammers into me with punishing force. Our bodies slap together, nothing but our heavy breaths passing between us. Roane grabs my leg, throwing it over his shoulder coming at me from an angle and holy fuck, I never knew a man could fuck me so deep. I feel like I'm losing my damn mind. My body quakes and trembles. Each new sensation better than the last.

Roane grins down at me knowing I'm close. He draws out slowly and beats his throbbing cock against my clit as it pulses with need. I reach down between us and grasp his shaft, rubbing the head over my sensitive nerves in a circle. Dipping his head down, his teeth skim over my taut nipple. Electricity shoots through me and stars dance behind my eyes, my orgasm takes over and I let out a whimper.

Roane flips me over on my stomach. I go into position. Head down, back arched, ass up. My sexy biker slams into me from behind, hand firm on my shoulder, driving into me relentlessly. The headboard knocks against the wall, sounding as though it's knocking on Heaven's door. Grunting hard and deep, he twitches, and his warmth fills me. His thrusts slow but he's not finished. Roane stays stuffed inside me, kissing my shoulder blades, growing hard all over again.

Roane fucks me slower this time, rocking into me tenderly. Fingertips feather light on my back. His lips press to my skin achingly soft. Then I realize what he's doing. Mapping my bruises and kissing them. Tears burn in the creases of my eyes, and I bite the pillow to stop from crying out at the sweetness of the gesture. Looming over me, he continues rocking into me, but when his lips meet my ear, we both freeze. "Gonna ask you once and you're going to tell me the truth. Who the fuck put their hands on your beautiful body out of hate?"

"It's nothing. You should see him." I try to laugh it off, but Roane isn't having it.

"I'll never hurt you, but if you don't give me the fuckin' truth..." he gets a firm hold on one of the globes of my ass and squeezes. "I'll spank it out of you."

"Please, Roane. I—" my voice cracks.

"Tell me now, Jules," he growls, and the dark tone is predatory.

"It's none of your business."

"Not my business." He draws out and slides back in. "You feel that. That's my come leaking out you. That's my dick buried deep in you. It became my business the moment you gave up your pretty pussy to me."

"Roane."

"I want a name." He pumps harder and faster. "I'll fuck it out of you." His hand leaves my ass and comes back in a playful smack, but I don't think he's in the mood to play.

"I'll tell you if you promise you won't tell Pam and you don't go being a hero."

"Fuck no. I'm telling you now, Jules. I want a name." His palm meets my ass again with more force this time that stings.

"Let me on top." I try changing the subject.

"You think you can fuck me into forgetting?"

"I can try."

"All right, baby doll. Give it your best shot." He spanks me again and we change positions.

I sink down on his cock in a reverse cowgirl. I can't look him in the eyes right now and he's already saw the bruises. Roane yanks on my hair, wrapping it around his fist. Bouncing on his thighs, I push away thoughts of Sam and replace those memories with the reality of Roane. Together we get lost for a while longer. With the promise of new beginnings and leaving the past year behind. I give myself to him and wonder if I can walk away from him a second time.

**

Blinking awake, I struggle to move. A warm, heavy body is pressed against me. A strong arm is curved around my waist, hand cupping my breast. An even stronger leg is draped over my thigh holding me captive. My head pounds from the liquor I ingested last night. Between my legs, my pussy aches. It went to battle with a big dick last night.

That massive monster belongs to Roane, the man who reminded me last night what it was like to be wanted and cherished. I struggle to slide out from under him, needing to find my clothes and a bathroom. The moment I move his hand it shoots right back to the same spot. "Hey," I whisper and try again.

"Stop moving," he grumbles. "Go back to sleep. It's early."

I glance around the room and look to the window seeing that it's still dark out. "I need the bathroom."

"Over there," he mutters and points to what I thought was a closet.

This time he lets me slide out of bed. I tiptoe across the room and wait until I'm on the other side of the bathroom door to flick the light on. It's a small half bath consisting of a toilet, medicine cabinet, and sink. I splash some water on my face and look in the mirror. My lipstick is smeared across my cheek and my eyes are ringed in black. My hair is a mess. What I need is coffee and a shower. I wonder if Pam is still here or if her and Link went home. I'm sure Roane or someone will give me a ride back to their place.

Finishing up in the bathroom after cleaning up the best I can, I return to the bed and find Roane awake and pushed up against the headboard with his arms crossed behind his head. He's even cuter than I remember. Blush blooms on my cheeks as memories of the night we shared rushes back to me.

"C'mere."

I drop onto the bed and curl up next to him. His fingers skate across my back, and I hiss. The soreness has returned. "I didn't forget about this you know. I'm not gonna make you tell me right now, but I promise you this, you will tell me, and I will make the fucker bleed for this."

"It's over."

"Way I see it. Shit is just getting started."

"Roane. You don't need to be my hero. You don't know me now. I've changed."

"Know you better than most people. Know how you feel when you come on my cock. Know the sounds you make when you like my tongue shoved deep in your pussy."

"You did not just say that."

"I did. And maybe your sister didn't tell you, but my brothers and I are fucking possessive bastards. You might have forgotten that about me, but I'm reminding you now. Not only are you Pam's sister but you gave me that pussy last night. We take care of our own. You were the first girl I ever loved, and I'm thinking I'd like to keep you."

"Keep me? I'm not property. I'm a person."

"Hate to break it to you, baby doll, but you're in The Devil's Playground. Normal rules don't apply."

"You're talking crazy."

"You gonna tell me you don't feel something between us? You gonna tell me you let just any man fuck you over and over again without a rubber?"

"No. We had unprotected sex. It was a lack of judgment. Two people caught up in the moment. That doesn't mean that you own me or that I'm beholden to you and whatever it is you think you're feeling. Are you still drunk?"

I like Roane and last night was great, but I'm

not stupid. I don't expect us to pick up where we left off when we were two kids fooling around.

Chapter 6

ROANE

"I'm being real with you. It's been three years since I've went down on a woman. Been three years since I've fucked someone without a rubber. Last woman I gave that to was my wife. She cheated on me, and I swore I'd never take another woman as mine, but when you walked in last night, I felt things I thought would be lost to me forever."

Fucking hell what's wrong with me spouting all this pussy bull shit? I don't do this. I don't get involved but right now Jules has me ready to beg her to give me a real shot. Sure, I first set out to fuck her, but as the night wore on shit got real. The moment I kissed her I knew, I felt it down in my damn bones that this woman was meant to be my forever. It was always supposed to be her.

I need to get my head on straight.

"Are you on birth control?" I should've asked her last night, but I was so damn wrapped up in the moment I never even stopped to think about it. I only wanted her.

"You're kind of freaking me out here."

"Answer the question."

"I think I need to go find my sister."

"I think you had better start talkin'."

"Newsflash. I don't owe you any explanations."

"Think you need to tell me if you're on the pill or not considering how many times I came inside you." I tighten an arm around her not wanting her to get out of this bed. I'm tempted to chain her to it until she gives in and agrees to what I want. I don't even know what all that is yet, I only know that I have her and I'm not letting go.

"I'm not having this conversation."

"The hell you aren't."

"I'm not worried about getting pregnant. I was with my ex for five years and it never happened for us."

"I'm not your ex and my swimmers are strong. Had that shit tested when my ex couldn't conceive. But you still didn't answer me. Are. You. On. The. Pill?"

"Why are you acting all crazy? Pam said you were cool to hook up with. That you wouldn't have expectations. Now I wake up and you're being all psycho on me and talking about feelings."

"Shit changed."

"When? How?" She laughs.

"The moment I had a taste of your mouth I fuckin' knew."

"Knew what?"

"That you're meant to be mine."

"Okay. I'm out of here. You know I didn't need any lines. You already got me into bed so I'm not sure what in the hell you're trying to pull here. I just left one crazy bastard. I don't need to get mixed up with another."

"I still want that name. If you don't give it to me, your sister will."

"I don't know what you want from me."

"Everything, I want it all, Jules. I want you."

"You don't know what you're saying."

"Fuck if I don't. Tell me you don't feel something when you look at me. Tell me that you felt nothing when you begged me to come in you again and again last night. How many times I fuck you last night, baby?"

"Stop it."

"Want that fucker's name."

"It doesn't matter. Why do you care so much?"

"Fifteen years ago, I fell in love with this feisty little cheerleader. She fuckin' drove me crazy. I couldn't do nothing but think of a future with her and then life happened, and she was taken away from me. Never stopped thinking about you, Jules."

"You could've asked Pam about me."

"I did. She always told me you were happy and gonna marry some lawyer. He the one that did this to you?"

"I don't want to talk about this. Can you just drive me to Pam's house?"

"No but I can chain you to my damn bed until you tell me why you're pushing me away."

"Last night was perfect. Let's not ruin it."

"Call me crazy all you want, but I'm not letting you go a second time. Don't you see it, sweetheart? Life is giving us a second chance."

"My life is messed up right now. I have things to take care of in Cleveland."

"And what do you have here? Your sister. People who love you. Me."

"You can't know that it'd work out."

"And you can't know that it won't. How long you in town for?"

"I'm supposed to drive back tomorrow."

"Give me till then."

"To do what?"

"Prove you belong here with me."

"You're absolutely mad, you know that?"

"Mad about you." I pull her back into my side and hold her. She doesn't fight me or try to argue but Jules is stubborn. I know her. She may think she's changed but deep down she's the same ol' Jules. The girl I've always loved.

Her belly rumbles.

"You hungry, baby doll?"

"I could eat."

"Get dressed. I'll take you out for breakfast then drop you back at Pam's so you can get ready."

"Roane."

"No ifs or buts about it. You said I have one day."

"I never agreed to that."

"I didn't ask. I'm telling you."

"You're impossible. You know that, don't you?"

"Don't act like you don't like me being a bossy asshole. It's been years, but I still know how to wet your panties. Now get dressed before I change my mind about the chains."

"Fine. You win."

"Get used to it."

She shakes her head and slides out of bed, picking her clothes up off the floor. I still haven't forgotten about them bruises on her back. Whoever the fucker is he's as good as dead.

Chapter 7

The man has lost his mind. I pull my jeans up and tug the sweater I had on last night over my head. He needs to get some food in him to soak up all the liquor. Once he gets awake and is thinking clearly, he'll get over whatever this is. Last night was perfect. Too good to be true. What are the odds of reconnecting with my high school boyfriend and things still burning bright as they did back then if not hotter? I can't afford to be impulsive.

The idea of Roane and I getting together after all these years is an attractive fantasy, but he can't know that we'd even be compatible or want the same things. Sure, I'd love to move here, but I need time to figure things out, and I can't just go hopping into a relationship with the first guy I've fucked since Sam. I ty to push Sam back out of my head. I do need to move out of our apartment, but I can't depend on Roane to save me. That's not fair. The last thing I want is him and his club going after Sam and getting into a world of trouble. I'm not bringing my troubles to their door. I'm a big girl. I've gotten this far on my own.

Roane comes out of the bathroom with his toothbrush hanging out of his mouth. "I'll be ready in a few."

"Take your time." Part of me wishes I could pretend the rest of the world doesn't exist and that I could disappear with Roane. Nothing in my life has ever been easy. I don't expect it start now. I sit on the edge of the bed and try not to imagine a life with Roane. A life where I'm his woman and I get to see my sister whenever I want to. I gave up on that fantasy years ago. That was child's play.

"Ready?" He shrugs his leather vest and jacket on.

"Mhmm." I get to my feet and slide my heels back on. Roane is staring at me like he wants to kiss me, but he doesn't make a move. Maybe he is finally coming to his senses about this. I follow him downstairs. Remnants of last night's party are scattered about along with random bodies on couches. Some are even on top of the pool tables and on the floor. We maneuver around them careful not to make too much noise.

When we get outside, he pulls his keys out and hits the unlock button on his truck. Like a gentleman he opens the passenger side door for me. I wait for him to get in the driver's side feeling like I did when we went on our first date. Nervous but excited. I was fifteen and he had recently gotten his driver's license. My Mom agreed to let him take me to the movies. It was such a big deal. It was my first time alone with a boy in a car. My first time going to the movies without the supervision of my sister.

Roane drives us to the drive-thru of Suzi's Hamburgers. I get an order of biscuits and gravy and he orders a BLT sandwich. "Hope you don't mind if we take breakfast to my place, I need to check on the shop."

"Shop?"

"Yeah. I have a tattoo place."

"I had no idea. That's really cool." He was always a talented artist so I shouldn't be surprised he makes a living from it.

"It's all right. So what do you do in Cleveland?"

"Hair. I'm a color specialist."

"You enjoy it?"

"It's a job."

"That's a no."

I shrug. "I don't know. It's fun. I hate being on my feet all day."

"You could come work for me."

"And what would that entail?"

"Answering the phone, keeping the place clean. Ordering supplies."

"You're serious?"

"I need someone."

I shake my head. "You're just saying that."

"Wouldn't ever lie to you." He holds my gaze, and something tells me that he wouldn't. Roane is a good guy under that tough man exterior. We pull into a parking lot and he shuts the truck off and hurries around to open my door. He's laying it on thick. Then again Roane was always sweet with me.

We go up a set of stairs connected to the back of a brick building. Roane unlocks the door and invites me inside to his apartment. It's more like a studio apartment. Entering behind him, he shows me to the kitchen that sits off the left. All nice stainless-steel appliances. The living room takes up the center of the room, housing a black leather sofa, a flat screen Tv, and a black and white portrait of I am assuming his motorcycle. There's some weights to the right along with two doors I assume lead to the bedroom and bathroom. It's clean and nice. Not that expected it to be a shithole. I know that some guys tend to be pigs when living on their own.

"Make yourself comfortable. You can eat at the counter or on the couch. I don't have room for a dining table. I've got to run downstairs to the shop. I'll only be a few minutes."

"Don't you want to eat?"

"I'll take it with me." He grabs his sandwich and leaves me on my own.

I take my food over to the couch and switch the Tv on. I don't know how long he'll be down there. I settle in on the cushions. He said he had been married and that she cheated on him. I can't imagine anyone doing that to him. She must be an idiot. I crumble my biscuits and pour the white gravy over them and dig in.

I stop flicking through the channels on HGTv. I love watching the flea market swap stuff. I throw my trash away, kick my shoes off, and get comfy on the couch with a pillow and throw that was hanging on the back.

"You like that shit?" Roane questions, startling me. I must've dozed off.

I sit up as he rounds the couch and pulls my feet up to slide in under them. Wiping my eyes, I whisper yawn, "Yeah, I do. I don't know I've always wanted to do that."

"Decorate?"

"Yeah. Refurbish furniture, paint. I don't know. It seems like it'd be fun to do."

"You're hired."

"For what? Stop trying to make up jobs for me."

"I need my place fixed up."

"It's fine."

"It's bare. I don't know I need some color. The touch of a woman." His fingers strum my ankle.

"I appreciate what you're trying to do. I do. I just...Roane, you can't really expect me to I don't know hop right into being with you, like there hasn't been fifteen years between us."

"I'm not asking. While you were sleeping, I got that name I wanted. As we speak, some brothers from the Cleveland chapter are packing your shit into a moving van and driving it down later today. Your stuff will be here tomorrow."

My mouth is on the floor. "You did what?"

"You heard me."

"You mean here as in this city or here as in this spot?"

Roane slides me forward into his lap. "I'm saying, I never much believed in fate until last night. You're here because it's where you've always belonged. I'm not taking any chances.

You're not slipping through my fingers a second time, baby doll."

"You're insane. I can't just move in with you, Roane."

"Says who?"

"Me!"

"Take a chance on me, Jules." His lips claim mine and I melt into him. I don't know what the hell I'm doing, but Roane was right. I do feel something for him. I always have. He was my first love.

This is it. My chance at a fresh start. It's completely mad, but life is too short, and I've wasted too much time playing it safe. Doing what I thought was right.

Chapter 8

ROANE

"**Y**ou said you were married."

"Yeah. Leah. Thought I loved her, but I think I was in love with the idea of her. Not who she really was. I should've known better. She was a hangaround at the club. Not Old Lady material. I was on the road a lot. She was home alone a lot and bored. Came home early one day and found her fuckin' the neighbor. I was mad at first, but the past three years have taught me that there was a part of me that was relieved."

"Sam cheated too," she confesses.

"He's a piece of shit."

"No argument here."

"I'm damn glad you're here."

"You know this is crazy? You've what been back around me for like twelve hours and you already want to move me in."

"Don't give a damn what anyone thinks. It feels right. I know what I want. What I've always wanted."

Before she can respond a knock sounds at the door.

"You expecting company?

"Something like that." Jules is going to be pissed but I did what I needed to. I get up and go to the door. As soon as I open it, Pam shoves past me.

"Where is she?"

Jules pops up. "Well hello, sister."

"I can't believe you. He fucking beat you and you didn't tell me shit all about it. I had to hear it secondhand through Roane when he called to ask questions. What. The. Serious. Fuck! I'm going to cut his balls off and feed them to him. No first I'm going to step on them with my stilettos. Then I'm going to start peeling his nails off. I swear. Sam is a dead man. Fucking dead." She stomps toward her sister. "Lift up your shirt."

"What? No." Jules gives me a death glare and I shrug. "Put a leash on her, Link."

Pam's head goes back as she cackles. "Real cute. He's pissed off at you too."

"Why?"

"For not coming to us. We're your family, Jules. If you can't count on us, then who has your back?"

"You're right. I should have told you. I'm sorry. So that's why you are going to hear this from me. I'm staying here. Roane has asked me to move in with him and I've accepted."

"You what? I mean damn, Roane. I asked you to look out for her, but don't you think that's a little rushed? Shouldn't you two be getting to know each other again. I mean I had hoped he'd convince you to stay, but this is I don't even know."

"It's what we both want. I fell in love with Jules back in the day and I never stopped caring about her. I love your sister."

Pam's lips spread into an evil smirk. "You love her? So my plan worked."

"Yeah. I do. What plan though?"

She rushes me, throwing her arms around me and kissing my cheek. "Thank you."

"Um…you're welcome." I look to Jules and she shrugs.

"I knew if I got you two back together last night sparks would fly. I didn't imagine it working so damn fast is all, but I know you'll treat her right. You always did."

Link is still being quiet. I know that look. He's plotting.

"So…," Pam starts. "How are we going to kill him?"

"No one is killing anyone. It's done and over. I'm here safe with you guys. I'm not going back."

"Gonna wrap a chain around his neck and drag him behind my bike," Link growls.

"Promise me you won't go after Sam. All of you."

"I promise you won't know when or what I do to the fucker but he's going to pay," I tell her.

"As much as I'd love to watch him get his, it's not worth it. He's not worth it. His father is a police officer. Sam won't take it lying down. He'd come at the club hard. I'm not dragging ya'll into my problems."

"I hear what you're saying, but I'm not afraid of that pussy or his daddy. Learn it now, Jules. There's gonna be shit I do you don't like. Gonna be shit you aren't allowed to question me on. You're gonna be my Old Lady and that's simply the way of it. When it's just you and me, baby doll, you can be as mouthy as you want, but when I'm with my brothers you don't open your mouth against me, understand."

"I hear you."

"I mean it, Jules. Not fuckin' around with this shit. It's important."

"I got it," she snaps, and I grin. There's her fire.

**

I didn't think Pam and Link were ever gonna go home. Love them both, but I just got Jules back, and I want her all to myself. She's taking a shower, and I'm kicked back on the couch smokin' a bowl. I need it to calm my ass down. All I can think about is that fucker putting his hands on her. I should have sent her home with Pam so I can go kill the sorry sack of shit. This shit has to be done right though, and I gotta talk to Murder. Let him know what's going down. I acted without running my call to Cleveland by him, but I did what I had to, and I'd do it again. It was my marker to collect. However, there is a protocol, and I didn't follow it. I'll answer to that tomorrow.

Jules walks out the bathroom with a towel on her head and one around her body. "You mind if I borrow a shirt? My stuff is at Pam's."

"What's mine is yours." I put my pipe on the coffee table. "That shirt can wait though. C'mere."

My girl pads softly across the room, stopping in front of me. I run my hands up the backs of her silky thighs. "I'm going to get you all wet," she protests as I discard the towel separating us.

"Don't care. I want to look at you." Moving my fingers over her curves, I inspect her for more bruises in the light. There's a few places on her thighs and uppers arms. Motherfucker put his hands on the wrong woman. "Gonna put my ink on you. Give you my property patch. Want everyone to know that I'm down for you. You're my queen. I adore you, Jules. Nobody will ever come

89

before you. I promise you that my love and my word is real."

"Roane," my name leaves her parted lips in a sweet whisper that caresses my cock. "I'm scared that this is all too good to be true."

"I get that, but I promise I'm going to prove it to you." I pull her down to my lap sealing my vow with a kiss. "Now give me that pussy." I stand up with her legs around me, arms cradling my neck, and take her to my bed.

Dropping my sexy girl gently on the covers, I drag her to edge, ass hanging off the bed. Down on my knees I pay worship to my queen. Tossing her legs over my shoulders, I cup her thick ass that I love so much, and I eat her good. I eat my woman until the balls of her feet press into my shoulders and her hips lift off the bed. Her sweet juices coat my tongue, her orgasm sending her over the edge. I get to my feet and slide right in that warmth finding paradise between her thighs.

Chapter 9

"Is it possible to die by way of orgasm?"

Roane's chest vibrates beneath my head as laughter erupts from deep in his belly. "Maybe we'll found out one day." His fingers skim along my arm. "You feeling relaxed and good now, baby doll?"

"Mhmm," I murmur, rubbing my fingers through his chest hair. I never thought chest hair was sexy, but Roane makes anything hot. I kiss his pec, sucking his nipple between my teeth and nipping him playfully.

"Good. Let's go downstairs and see about that ink."

I tense up. "Right now?" I've feared needles since I was a kid. I love tattoos and think they are beautiful it's just the thought of the needle that ruins the whole idea.

"You don't want my ink on you?" I can hear it in his tone. I've wounded his pride.

"It's not that trust me. I don't expect you'd remember everything, but needles scare the shit out of me."

"Well don't go shitting the bed, sweetheart. I'm not into skat play."

I punch him in the stomach lightly. "Into what?"

"You don't want to know."

"I'll take your word for it."

"Come on. I'm taking you to dinner then we'll talk more about that ink."

"I don't have anything to wear."

"We'll drop by Pam's and you can change. We can see if her and Link want to join us."

My face lights up. "Really?"

"Yeah, I'd do anything to keep that look right there on your face." My cheeks are pink, colored in happiness. Lips stretched upward, curving into a bright smile. All because of this man. "Happy looks real good on you, Jules."

"Being here with you...it does make me happy. Getting to be near Pam...it's all great. I only hope that my situation doesn't make you feel pressured into something you aren't ready for. I know I could stay with Pam until I get on my feet."

"Stop. Don't look for excuses to discount the way I feel about you. I wouldn't have called in a favor to get all your shit here so fast if I wasn't serious about this. About us."

"I'm trying. Be patient with me."

"We have forever, baby doll." His words reassure me, and I slide out of bed and shimmy back into my dirty jeans I borrowed from my sister. Roane gives me one of his long-sleeved Harley tees. It swallows me but it smells like him, making it perfect.

I keep thinking that any minute now I am going to wake up and this whole weekend will have been nothing but a dream. What are the odds that I'd end up in bed with my high school sweetheart on New Year's? This sort of thing never happens in real life. It's the sort of story you read about online or see in a movie, but these types of good lucky things, don't just happen to me. I'm trying to embrace it and roll with things as they come but there's this voice nagging in the back of my mind that sounds a lot like Sam telling me that Roane could never love my fat ass and that I don't deserve to be happy.

He drives us over to Pam and Link's. This is what I have always wanted. My man and my sister's man being good friends. Sam wouldn't be caught dead hanging with the likes of Link based on his appearance alone. He's rough around the edges.

Roane is out in the garage smoking and having a beer with my brother-in-law while I get changed and my sister talks my ear off.

"I gotta say, Sis. You sure shocked the hell out of me. I thought for sure I'd have to twist your arm to get you to agree to move home, but all I needed was Roane to give you that mega dick." She howls with laughter.

The woman is a damn cracker jack. "Shut up. I can't believe it either really. It's surreal. I feel like an imposter living someone else's life to be honest."

"So what kind of tattoo you think he's going to give you?"

My stomach drops. All color washes from my face.

"Relax. Nothing to fear. Roane does great work. You won't feel a thing. If you're scared about hearing the buzzing sound of the gun, we can put you some headphones in and play you relaxing sounds or some shit. Light soothing candles. Whatever you need. Smoke a joint. Just saying."

"Only you."

"Let's go eat. I'm starving after the workout Link gave me last night."

"I don't need to know the details of your sex life."

"Oh whatever." She loops her arm through mine. "I have to know. Did Roane live up to his reputation?"

I make the motion of locking my lips and throwing away the key.

"Don't you dare. Tell me everything. Well okay not everything but is he really that big?" She holds her hands apart guessing his size.

"Bigger. Much bigger." I giggle as her brown eyes widen.

"Well damn. And you ain't even walkin' funny. My baby sister is a ho."

"You aren't wrong. The things he can make me do..." I bump my hip against hers and we both laugh.

I end up driving my car to the restaurant, so we don't have to swing back by Pam's for it later. We end up at a pizza joint and arcade. One I used to come to after school when we dated.

"C'mere and look at this." Roane motions me to a wall of photographs and points. There's a picture of us. His arm is around me and we both have the cheesiest grins plastered on our faces. I lean into him and he pecks my lips with a soft kiss. "You and I were always meant to be, baby doll."

"You think so?"

"I know so. C'mon. Let's order."

I slide into the booth next to my man and I can't help but embrace the giddy feeling washing over me. This is what I've been missing. Roane. Pam. Even Link.

This is right.

He's right.

I belong with Roane.

**

"You ready for this?" Pam stands behind the chair in Roane's shop ready to hold my hand if needed.

Roane is taking his sweet time sketching a unique design. He does this for every client.

He doesn't do the same tattoo twice. He goes through all the prep steps and I put in headphones, turning my playlist up loud to drown out the sound, I close my eyes. I'm unable to watch. If this wasn't so important to him, I wouldn't be going through with this. The last time I had blood drawn I fainted on the spot. I feel a small stinging sensation and it's not as bad as I imagined. The process takes longer than I'd like but it definitely could be worse.

After an hour and a half, Roane's lips press against mine. He pulls an earbud out and I open my eyes. "All done. You did great. Come look in the mirror before I bandage your wrist."

It's a black and grey shaded lotus flower with tribal patterned leaves and his name around it. It's beautiful.

"The lotus is a sign of rebirth, the leaves represent growth, and I think my name is obvious."

"I love it. Thank you." I cup his furry jaw and go in for a kiss. His tongue probes deep and wet against mine. The way this man kisses ought to be a crime. So good. I pull back realizing I don't hear my sister's sassy mouth. "Where's Pam?" I look around for my sister.

"Her and Link had to get to the clubhouse. She said she'd see you tomorrow. Let's get you bandaged so we can go up and get ready for bed."

"Sounds good to me." I help Roane clean up after he bandages my tattoo. "Did you mean it that you wanted my help with managing your shop?"

"Yup."

"Wouldn't you get sick of spending so much time with me?"

"Never." His arms come around me, cupping my backside and giving me a squeeze.

Chapter 10
ROANE

Jules is at the bathroom sink brushing her teeth. Having her here, makes me realize what I've been missing. Someone to share my life with. I thought I was good with being single but now that I have her, I know I was simply coasting through from one day to the next. Fucking random women whenever the need arose never finding satisfaction. A physical release. But no sense of real joy in the act.

Jules is the real deal. The kind of woman you grab onto and hold on to no matter the costs. I know she's been hurt, but I'll build her back up. I finish up in the shower and wrap a towel around my waist. I step behind her, wrapping my arms around her. Nothing better than holding her besides being buried deep within her. I noticed her wincing in pain earlier and made her take some painkillers for that tattoo and her back.

Kills me to think of my girl hurting because that low life laid his fists on her body. He's going to learn that he messed with the wrong woman. Link made me promise that whenever I take him out that I'll let him get some licks in. He cares about Jules too being she's his sister-in-law. "You ready for bed?"

"Mhmm." She takes her earrings out, placing them off to the side.

I kiss her shoulder, tempted to bend her over the sink and fuck her right here. "Tomorrow when your stuff arrives, Pam is gonna come over to help you unpack. I want you to put your things wherever you want. This is your place as much as its mine. If you have stuff that won't fit or that needs stored there's a spare room in the back of the shop you can use that has a door that locks on it. It'd be safer there than one of the storage units."

"Okay. Sounds good to me. I don't have a lot. Mostly my wardrobe and a few knickknacks that belonged to my Nee-nee."

"Let me at the sink." She moves off so I can brush my teeth and finish up. By the time I've finished and go to get in bed she's already passed out, having claimed the left side. It's the side I normally sleep on but I'm not gonna complain. I'm merely happy to share my bed with her. I slide in under the covers and align my body with Jules', hugging her from behind. One arm over her chest and a leg thrown over hers. She curves into me, that thick ass pushed up on me.

Fucking hell, the warmth and touch of my woman is making me hard again, but I'm not going to wake her. She needs sleep. We both do.

I close my eyes, but all I can focus on is that curvy body pressed into mine like a perfect fit. Sliding a hand under her shirt, I palm her tit, teasing the rosy nipple, rolling the sensitive skin between my thumb and finger until it hardens to a point and my sexy vixen is moaning.

"Shouldn't you be sleeping," her voice is whispery and soft.

"Can't keep my hands to myself." My lips drag along the slender column of her neck. Jules rolls to her back and I move over top her. She's wearing these drawstring pants that are pulled too tight for me to get at her. "You trying to keep me out?"

She laughs. "No, trying to keep my pants up. They're a size too big."

I grunt. "Don't want you wearing shit all to bed. Want to be able to take you anytime I want to."

"Well considering its winter and I get cold easily, that's not happening." Her feet press into my calves.

"Damn, baby doll. What you do, stick them things in the freezer before you got into bed?" I dip my head to claim those lips.

"You caught me."

"Want some socks?"

107

"I'd just kick them off."

"Why don't you kick these off," I suggest, yanking on the knotted strings separating me from what I need. I push her shirt up over her head, getting an eyeful of her perfect tits. Her nipples are erect in desperate need of being sucked. I take my time paying attention to both, alternating between the two. Lips parting, the pace of her breathing increases. So damn responsive. I thrust my hips, wanting her to feel how hard she has me. "Need these pants out the way, Jules."

Reaching between us she undoes the knot and starts shoving the thick cotton down her thighs. She gets them part way down before I slam inside her. Goddamn, she's so fuckin' wet, my cock slides right in. Squeezing me tight, she nearly has me coming for her already. The woman has voodoo pussy. Pussy so damn good it must be cursed.

"You've completely ruined me. Destroyed my cock for anyone else. Nothing better than this, Jules."

"Good," she whispers and takes all I have to give.

**

"He give you any trouble?"

"Pansy ass motherfucker nearly shit his pants when he opened the door and saw Sledge and me on the other side," Sleeper tells me. "Threatened to call his cop daddy. That shit made me laugh. I wanted to beat the fuck out of him but did as you asked, left him without a hair touched." He laughs and pulls a cigarette out.

"Good. I don't want any blowback on anyone. That asshole will never see me coming."

"Heard that."

"Help me unload the truck then we'll ride over to the clubhouse."

Jules went to lunch with Pam. The guys and I get the boxes packed upstairs and stacked in the living room. The two of them can sort through her stuff and unpack when they return. I have to check in with Prez and let him know about that piece of shit Sam.

Murder is already expecting us when we arrive at The Devil's Playground. He's seated at his reserved table drinking some Black Rebel Riders' MC apple pie moonshine. I recognize the label on the jar. He kicks a chair and mutters, "Have a seat." I take the seat next to him and Sleeper and Sledge borrow chairs from neighboring tables. "You boys doin' some sightseeing?"

"I called in a marker."

"Wanna tell me why I'm just hearing this?"

"Had to make a move. Pam's sister, Jules is in town. Me and her have history. Long story short the bastard she was with been beating on her, and I called Sleeper to go to her place and pack her shit up. They drove the truck down and delivered her belongings."

"You claiming her I take it?"

"Put my ink on her last night."

Murder shakes his head and takes a hefty drink. "What of the boyfriend?"

Sleeper speaks up. "Left him untouched but did some digging. Made some calls. Fucker wears a suit. Thinks his shit smells like roses. Lawyer with a cop daddy into dirty shit. Takes bribes. The son has some bad habits and owes the Cortez Cartel for a lot of blow. Word is he's on the hook bad. He won't be around long. Mikal is not a patient or understanding man."

"I'll put in a call and set up a meeting. I'll buy his debt if they deliver him to the warehouse breathing," Murder decides. "Then we'll show him what we do to spineless pricks who hurt women." he looks to me. "That good with you?"

"Yeah, Prez. Sounds good to me. As long as I get watch him take his final breath."

Chapter 11

Pam eyes the stacks of boxes that have taken over Roane's living room. "Shit. It's official, little sister. Welcome to the Old Ladies' Club."

"The what?"

"You know. You're officially one of the girls. Us Old Ladies stick together. We get together once a week for girl's night. We each take turns hosting. I won't add you to the rotation until you and Roane get settled in. I'm still shook he asked you to move in so fast. You musta' gave it to him good." Her tongue darts out wagging like a dog's tail.

"Is sex all you think about? You're worse than a man."

"No shame in my game. I'm a sexual being and comfortable with talking about it."

I roll my eyes. "Take this to the bathroom." I hand her the box of my toiletries. I have to give Roane's friends credit they were thorough and took everything. Even the toilet paper. "I'll sort through it later. Right now I just want to get the boxes to their designated area."

My summer clothes and shoes will have to go downstairs for storage. Roane has like twenty pairs of jeans hanging in his closet. The space is definitely limited. I start moving my winter clothes into the bedroom when my sister comes out of the bathroom swinging a big ol' flesh colored dildo around.

My eyes go big and round. "Where the hell was that?"

"It was in your box." She grins. "I didn't know you were so kinky."

Cheeks flaming red and hot, I squeak out, "That's not mine."

"Eww." She flings the toy, and it rolls across the hardwood floor, coming to a stop at my feet. "Well if it doesn't belong to you then who?" She sticks her tongue out making a gagging sound.

"Hell if I know. I've never seen that thing in my life. You better wash your hands. Who knows where it's been? Do you think those guys would have stuck it in there as a joke?"

"I guess it's possible, though playing pranks isn't really Sleeper's style from what I know of the dude. I've only met him a handful of times at rallies. Do you think it was Sam's?"

"Sam? No way." I shake my head, however I also never thought Sam would cheat on me or develop a drug problem. At first, he said he only wanted to have a little fun. Said it was part of being in the boys' club at work.

Whatever that meant. I never thought he'd attack me either. Looking back, it's as though I was living with a complete stranger. This time though things will be different. I know Roane and he knows me. With him its easy and natural. Nothing forced. We click. We fit, like two halves of one whole. "I don't know but I'm getting rid of it." I go into the kitchen and find a drawer stuffed full of plastic bags. I use one to pick the toy up and the other to discard it in.

"I'm going to go bleach my hands."

"I'll be back. I'm just gonna go toss this in the dumpster."

"Sure...have fun taking the trash out. It's okay, Julie. You're a woman and allowed your kinks."

"Seriously? So help me I will give it to Link and tell him you want him to shove it in your you know what."

"Don't threaten me with a good time."

"You're impossible."

"I'm unforgettable, darling," she mocks.

I slip my furry boots and my hoodie on. I'm only going downstairs and back, but it's colder than a witch's tit out there. I hurry down the steps, the chill of the winter air nipping at my cheeks. The sky is gray. The weatherman gave a forecast of snow for later this evening. It's a perfect evening to cook chili and curl up with Roane and watch a movie.

We have so much ahead of us. So many new memories to make. A week ago, the thought of love seemed laughable. Now I can't imagine anything but him. It's all happening so fast, but I know he's it for me. I had always thought about him over the years. Wondering what happened to him and if he had a family. I never thought he'd be a member of the same motorcycle club as my brother-in-law let alone be a biker at all.

To be fair though he always had a bad boy edge to him. It's what attracted me to him in the first place. Dark hair, even darker eyes. Warm tan skin and a mouth sweet like cinnamon sugar. He was my world then and he is quickly becoming my world now. A bolt of lightning shot straight through to my heart the moment our eyes met in the clubhouse.

Lost in my thoughts of him, I don't notice the tall figure lurking behind me until it's far too late. Opening the lid to the green dumpster, I drop the bag in and the moment I close it, a thick arm snakes around my throat, restricting my airway. Before I can scream another hand presses a cloth over my nose and mouth. Eyes rolling back in my head, I slump into the man's hold on me and before all fades to black I recognize the scent of his cologne. Woodsy with a hint of vanilla. Sam.

**

Coming to, I blink my eyes. My temples pulsing, throat dry, hands and feet bound together. Fabric covers my mouth, tightly fastened around the back of my head, biting into my ears. I roll to my side and there he is. Sam is seated at a table drinking a bottle of scotch and smoking a cigar. Lines of cocaine on the table. I still, not wanting him to notice that I'm awake. Fear lances through my veins. I don't know what he has planned or what he is even doing here. Why couldn't he let me go? He didn't love me. He said so himself.

It's only been a week since I last saw him and yet he looks differently now. Had I been blind to the physical changes in him? How skinny he has gotten. How hollow his cheeks are? How dead his once vibrant eyes are. He's not the man I cared about. This Sam is someone different. A man I don't recognize. A man I want nothing to do with.

I need to try and break free of these bindings.

He takes another swig from the bottle and curses under his breath. Head swinging toward me, he mutters more unintelligible mumblings. I close my eyes and pray he doesn't realize I've moved. He's drunk and high. Which means he is also going to be one mean bastard. I focus on breathing evenly and wonder how long I was unconscious for. Has Pam realized I'm missing? Of course she has. My sister is a nut, though I know the minute she realized I didn't return she called Link and Roane. They'll be looking for me, but will they find me before it's too late?

Chapter 12

Sam

The minute that biker trash left my place with the fat whore's things I got in my car and followed them. They had no clue. I followed them to West Virginia. I thought Julie would be at her sister's place but turns out she's been with some dumb bastard who doesn't know what a stupid cunt he's invited into his life. I watched them kissing and fawning over one another. Julie is mine. She belongs to me. I allowed her to go visit her skanky sister so she could see that I can be kind.

It was meant to be her last visit. We're not over till I say we're over and I didn't say. Julie is going to learn her lesson. No one questions me. No one tells me who to fuck and when. I've supported her fat ass for years. She was skinny when we first got together but as the years went on her hips got wider. I bought her gym membership and she wasted it. Said the place made her uncomfortable because the men stared at her body and hit on her. That was the point. I wanted them to look at what they couldn't have. See what I had. I need a beautiful woman on my arm when I make my run for office. She ruined those plans. I couldn't marry her. She wouldn't do. I needed to find a replacement for her and when the time was right, I was going to sell Julie to Mikal Cortez to pay off my debt. For some reason beyond my comprehension, he thought she was worth something.

I'm still going to make the deal but not until I've had my fun with her first. She has no clue how many times I've done this to her while she was sleeping. Drugged her and had my thrill. I've even let my old man have a go at her a few times. She'd wake up disoriented and sore, having no clue it was because I did whatever I wanted with her. I prefer her unconscious but this time I want to hear her screams. I want her to remember my face and feel my hands around her throat. I'd kill the bitch if I didn't need her as payment.

I snort two more lines. My nose burns and my eyes water as euphoria travels through my brain. I drink my scotch, hoping to be able to stomach seeing Julie naked again. It's pathetic that I have to get drunk and high to want to fuck her. I look over at her. Bound on the bed. My cock barely twitches at the sight. Shoving my chair back, I grip the edge of the table. My head feels swimmy. I shake the sensation off and go to her, undoing my pants to stroke myself in an attempt to get hard. I leave my pants to the floor of the cheap motel room and get into bed with her. She doesn't budge and I flip the Tv on and rent a movie to get me in the mood to play with her.

I watch the erotic film and touch myself. Now that I'm getting hard, I shake Julie to rouse her awake. "Wake up, bitch." I go up on my knees and smack my dick across her face. "There you are," I coo when her eyes pop open. "Did you really think you could ever leave me?" I laugh and remove the handkerchief I had tied over her mouth to gag her.

"You know they'll kill you for this," she hisses.

"Who, your biker trash?" I squeeze her face. "They'll have to find us first. I would tell you to suck me, but I don't trust you with your teeth. So you'll just have to lay there for what I have planned." I go in for a kiss and the dumb cunt tries to bite me earning her a punch to the face. She cries out and I get harder. "That's it scream for me, Julie. No one can hear you."

"Fuck you."

"Oh, I'm going to fuck you and then I'm going to give you to a friend who will use you up. Put you to work in one of his whore houses overseas. You'll be so drugged up you won't know your own name."

"What did I ever do to you, Sam? What happened to you? This isn't you. You aren't a rapist or woman beater."

"You don't know anything. Do you know all those times you woke up feeling like shit, it's because I drugged you. Even let my old man fuck you a few times too while I watched." Her face goes ashen and I smile. "That's right. All those times you felt weird around him. Felt his eyes moving over your body. Every time he licked his lips while watching you, it was because he was remembering how you tasted. Personally, I don't know what he found so appealing about your fat ass."

"You're lying."

"Am I, Julie? Am I? You think long and hard about that."

"You're sick."

"Enough of your mouth." I ball the handkerchief up and shove it between her teeth. I won't get to hear her scream, but her muffled cries will have to suffice. I flip her onto her back and push her shirt up. "You always did have nice tits." Her body jerks but she's not going anywhere, and neither am I until I get what I came here for.

To teach this cunt a lesson she'll never forget.

Chapter 13

ROANE

"How the hell you ask a bitch to be your Old Lady and move in with you after one night?" Crawl shakes his head at me.

"Brother, when you meet the one, you'll understand."

"It's true," Link agrees with me.

"Shit, does Pam have another sister?"

"Nope."

"Of course she doesn't." He takes a drink of his beer then lights up a cigarette.

Link's cell phone rings and he frowns. "It's Pam." He grunts and shoves back from the table, answering her call. "You never call me.

What's wrong? Slow down I can't understand you. What do you mean Julie disappeared?" He holds the phone out from his ear, and I jump up at his words.

"What's she saying about Jules?"

"I'm putting you on speaker phone. Yeah. Roane is right here. Go slow and talk clearly." He puts it on speaker, and we all listen in.

Pam is hysterical and it's hard to make out half of what she's saying. "Julie walked outside, and she never came back."

"The fuck you mean she never came back. Where are you?" I growl.

"Your apartment. I was in the bathroom and she was taking something to the dump. She said she'd be right back her purse and keys are here."

"What about her cell phone?"

"I tried calling it but no response."

"Fuck. We're heading that way now." I look at Sleeper. "Get someone to that apartment and see if that fucker left town."

"On it," he says, pulling his phone out.

"I'll let Prez know," Crawl starts down the hall to Murder's office.

"I told Pam to get Jules' cell number to Prodigy. He'll find her."

Murder comes rushing out of his office. "Let's go get the son'bitch." He's thinking the same as I am. Her ex made a move. One that is going to cost him his life.

My brothers and I ride out. Some to my place. Some are going to scout locations he may have taken her to. I don't know why but something tells me he hasn't left the area with her. It's a gut feeling I have.

When I get to my apartment Pam rushes into Link's arms snotting around. I don't pay her no mind. I am eager to pull up the security footage in the shop. I have cameras on the front and inside, but I also have them monitoring the back door to my business and my apartment. It doesn't take me long to find what I want. On one of the back cameras, I see everything. Jules' hurrying down the steps with a plastic bag. As she is throwing it away the fucker jumps her from behind and drugs her before she has a chance to fight back or cry for help. I watch powerlessly as he drags her to his car. The way it's parked I can't see the tags, but I know the make. I fire off a text to Prodigy.

My phone rings back immediately with a call from him. "What you got?"

"Got a ping on her phone. South side of the city. I'd bet my life he took her to Super 8."

"Thanks, man."

"Anytime. Go get your..." I end the call before he finishes. I'm already walking out the door.

I lift my chin to Link. "Super 8, south side."

Pam tries to come with us, but Link tells her to stay put. "That's my sister! This isn't the time for your macho club shit. I need to be there."

His gaze snaps to her. "Woman, stand your ass down so we can do what needs to be done. Don't make me spank your ass. You won't like the act of it this time."

Pam's mouth snaps shut for once. She knows her man means business. We don't need her coming along and being all hysterical. We don't know what we're riding into.

Murder joins up with us on the ride over along with Viking and Crawl. This motherfucker is going to regret the day he ever messed with what's mine. I roll to a stop a block away. I don't want the prick to know I'm coming though if he were smart, he'd be expecting me.

"This is your rescue, son. We'll follow your lead," Prez tells me and I give him a chin lift.

Our group enters the lobby of the motel and the short, fat, balding man swallows hard. "I don't want no trouble."

"There won't be any as long as you tell me what I want to know. I need the room number for a Sam Mueller."

"I'm not supposed to give that out."

I take a step forward and so do my brothers.

The man shrinks back. He clicks something on his computer. "Room 115." He slides a door key across the counter and Link pulls out his wallet. He tosses a few hundreds on the counter.

"Thank you for your time. You never saw us. Understood."

"Yeah. Yeah. Never saw you." He hurries to slip the money in his pocket.

It doesn't take long to find the room. It's down the hall on the first floor. My first instinct is to the kick the door down. Rage fills me when I hear moans echoing from the room.

"Easy, brother. Could be the wrong room," Murder tells me, placing a hand on my shoulder.

"Harder," a voice filters through the door followed by an even louder moan.

I shake my head and listen closer. "It's not her." I insert the plastic card into the door and when the green light flashes, I push it open.

I go in first followed by my brothers, I draw my handgun from my boot and train it on Sam. I recognize him from the security footage. He's naked from the waist down, wrestling on the bed with Jules. A porno flick is playing on the Tv. Sick fucker is going to meet his end at my hands. Her knees draw back, and she kicks him in the stomach. The two of them haven't even noticed the rest of us filling the room. Sam rolls off the bed, and I step over him to press the barrel between his brows.

"Don't move, you sorry sack of shit."

"Fuck you. Do it. I'm dead either way." He must be talking about his debt to the cartel.

"You don't get to take a coward's way out." I nod to Viking and Crawl to restrain him. They get ahold of him while I tend to Jules. He's put his hands on her again and just for that I'm going to make his death very slow and fucking painful. I'll drain the life from him so damn slow he'll pray for my mercy but never receive it.

Chapter 14

Roane caresses my cheek and I flinch at his light touch. It's been a few days since Sam kidnapped and attacked me. He left me with a busted, lip, bruised cheek, and blackened eye. Once my man knew I was battered but okay I thought he was going to beat Sam to death. It took Murder, Crawl, Link, and Viking to pull him off him and then Link went after him.

I don't know what became of Sam, but Pam told me it involved a chain and a motorcycle. She also said they handled his father. Whatever happened I'm simply glad he's gone — that they both are gone and that it's over. He won't be coming back, and Roane and

I can move on with our lives. Maybe that makes me seem cold and unfeeling, but Sam had no love for me. He had no problem hurting me.

I am only glad that my cell phone happened to be in the pocket of my hoodie and that Roane's brother Prodigy was able to track it so quickly. If not for him I may not be here on the couch with my man. He's been so attentive. So loving. Sweeter than I could have ever hoped for in a man.

"Can I get you anything?"

"I'm good. I have you. That's all I need."

"You sure you're up for the party tonight? Everyone will understand if you want to stay in."

"No way. I want to go. We need some fun. I'm ready to get to know the club and thank the guys who helped you rescue me."

Roane smiles and gives me a gentle kiss being careful not to hurt me. I've been a bit jumpy the past few days after what happened and the things that Sam said to me. I have no idea whether he was telling the truth or not. I keep telling myself he only said those things about his father to scare me. If I believe otherwise I will only spiral into a depression. I don't want that. Some people might say it's unhealthy to ignore it and try to forget what he said. Maybe it is but I only want to look to the future.

I have a bright one ahead of me.

"Good. Go get ready." My sexy man gives my ass a squeeze.

We haven't had sex since the attack. I know it's only because he worries about me, but I want him. I'm hoping if I get him relaxed enough, he will stop treating me like I am going to shatter whenever he touches me. I appreciate him being delicate and sensitive to my needs I do. But I have other needs too and I miss him.

What can I say? I'm addicted to Roane.

I pull his face back to mine and claim his lips. When he moves back, I gaze deeply into his eyes, and I know that he's my forever. A part of me has always known he was my one.

All it took for both of us was one kiss to seal our fate.

"I love you, Roane."

"Love you too, baby doll."

I go to the bedroom and lay out my clothes on the bed. My sweet nutty sister unpacked everything for me. She was feeling guilty because she was here when Sam grabbed me but neither of us had any way of knowing he would show up and do what he did. In the bathroom I get the shower ready and undress.

I'm not under the spray of water long before my man is stepping in behind me. "Holy shit, woman. What are you trying to do melt my balls off? Fuck that's hot."

"It's not that hot."

"The hell it isn't. Satan himself would be sweating."

"You don't have to showier with me," I point out, but I adjust the temperature a smidge.

"And miss out on seeing you all soaped up and naked. Not happening. I've missed you, Jules."

"I've been right here. You've not left my side," I remind him. He's been hovering over me like a helicopter and I've loved every second of it.

"No, I've missed this." His arm snakes around my waist, his hand dropping down to my pelvis.

"Oh." I smile when his fingers tease at my clit.

"Yeah. Oh. Need you, baby doll." *I hope he gives me a big O.*

"You've got me, Roane. Always and forever."

"I want us to make it official." His lips meet the back of my neck.

"We just moved in together."

"What's that got to do with it?"

He has a point. "Not a damn thing." I turn into him, seeking his mouth out. "Let's do it."

"Yeah?"

"Yeah."

My man comes alive, pushing me up against the tiled wall of the shower. Roane comes at me hard and fast, tongue plunging deep in my mouth, greedy and sexy. My man makes love to my mouth with his kiss. A kiss that promises me one thing—forever.

**

Three months later

"What'd you want to tell me, baby doll?" Roane stares up at me as I straddle him on the couch.

"That you were right."

"Hmm..." he grunts. "I'm always right."

"Are you now?" I roll my hips.

Roane reaches around me to squeeze my ass. "Fuckin' love your ass, Jules."

I lick my lips and move in closer to whisper in his ear. "There's one thing in particular you were right about." He shifts his hips and thrusts his growing erection upward, rubbing it through his sweatpants up against my crotch. "Stop distracting me. I'm trying to be serious."

"You're the one being all tempting in these tight ass pants, woman. Now tell me what I was right about."

"So bossy and demanding." I lick the shell of his ear and he chuckles.

"You call me distracting. You love to torture me."

"Hmm. Where was I? Oh yeah. I wanted to tell you that what you said about your swimmers being strong...you were right." I lean back so I can get a good look at his face when he realizes what I just revealed to him. He stares at me for a hot minute and blinks twice. Then it hits him and his lips fan into a gorgeous smile. One I know that is only for me.

"You saying what I think you're saying?"

"Yeah, honey. I am. We're pregnant." I've barely gotten the words out before his mouth is on mine.

Roane pulls back and I feel breathless. Every time I kiss him its magical, just like the first time. After things died down and we settled into life as a couple, Roane and I tied the knot on Valentine's day. The anniversary of our first kiss. The day he told me something I had forgotten about until he reminded me in his vows. "I swore I'd be your first and last kiss, Jules. I was the first man to ever kiss you when you were fifteen and I'll be the last when you're old and gray. I promise I'm going to cherish and love you for all of my days." Then he kissed me, and the preacher yelled at him for jumping ahead of the ceremony.

"God, you make me happy, woman."

"I can make you even happier if you take me to bed."

"Let's test that theory." He shifts to carry me to bed when a knock sounds at the front door then my sister let's herself in. "Thought I told you to start locking that door," he grumbles.

"Oops." I slide down his front.

"Am I interrupting?" Pam shoots Roane a cheeky grin knowing damn well and good she is.

"Go home, Pam," he barks, and I smack at his chest.

"Don't be rude. I want to share this moment with my sister."

"Uh, no offense, Jules. I know I joke around and shit, but I am not joining you two or watching."

"Eww fuck no," Roane growls.

"I'm pregnant," I tell her, and she squeals coming at both of us for a hug as she starts to cry.

"I'm going to be an Auntie?"

"Yeah, but get gone so I can get back to what I was doing before you interrupted." Roane loves my sister, honest, but she drives him bat shit crazy because she pops up all the time at random hours. He might as well get used to it. She is only going to get worse once the baby comes.

"Fine. I know when I'm not wanted. I only came by to see if Roane wanted in on the bet the guys got going."

"And what bet would that be?" he questions her.

"Oh…only that Wylla Mae is eighteen and graduating high school soon…we have a pool going to see how long it takes East to break."

"Ya'll, that is so damn mean. You ain't even right."

Pam shrugs and Roane says, "What dates you got left and what's the buy in?"

I shake my head at both of them, but I love them more than anything. "Fine. I am going to call it now and say one month after she's out of school they become a thing officially."

Pam smirks at me and Roane chuckles.

"See. You are one of us." My sister giggles and hugs my neck.

Roane places his bet and shoves her out the door daring her to come back until at least three days have passed.

"Why three days?"

"Because that's how long I plan on keeping you naked in bed."

"Oh, I like that. I like it a lot." I start sauntering toward the bedroom, shedding my clothes along the way so my man can make good on his promise and oh does he ever.

Author's Note

Dear Reader,

I hope you enjoyed this fun holiday story that centered on Roane and Jules. I wanted this story to serve as an introduction to the characters of my chapter of the Royal Bastards MC, Charleston West Virginia. Lady & the Biker is coming your way soon. It is a full-length novel. I cannot wait to share East and Wylla Mae's journey with you. Until then I have included a sneak peek of their book, I hope you enjoy it. If you loved reading about Roane and Jules, I hope you consider leaving a review.

Glenna

Preview of Lady & The Biker

Chapter 1

Easton

Rolling up behind Murder outside of the rundown two-story home a bad feeling passes over me. The older man kills his bike and motions for me to do the same. *Fuck.* He said he had to make a quick stop. Walking up on the porch of the two-story with white outdated siding, this doesn't feel fast to me. I scrub a hand over my face and make note of the boards nailed over the window and the bag of garbage that the cats or a dog has scattered across the front lawn.

Prez knocks twice. The patter of footsteps sounds and the dingy white door creaks open. He pushes it wider and enters. I follow behind him, and he squats to talk to a little girl who is sitting on the floor in front of a Tv watching cartoons. She's a tiny thing with hair so light it's almost white.

"What'd I tell you about opening the door without asking who it is first?"

The kid sniffles and wipes her hand across her nose. "Sorry," her angelic voice says in a low tone.

"Where's your mom? I picked up your prescription." Murder pats her on the head. He turns to me and hands me the white and blue bag from the pharmacy. "Give this to the kid," he gruffly orders me and stomps up the stairs.

"You sick or something?" Her warm brown eyes widen as she takes me in. I don't get a reply. Ripping the bag open I pull out a bottle of pink liquid. "What's your name, Lil' Lady?"

"Wylla Mae," she tells me with a sniffle then coughs.

I measure out the dosage and hand the plastic cup to her. "Drink it all down." I glance at the bottle and it says it needs refrigerated. The kid follows me to the kitchen. When I open the fridge door up and see that it's bare inside, I go tense. Not even a package of bologna. Anger courses through me. No way for a kid to be living. Shit like this burns me up. I may not be much but I'm not heartless. I look around the kitchen. The dishes are stacked by the sink and covered in flies. My stomach coils at the sight and the smell of the rotten food overflowing from the garbage can and onto the floor. Murder stomps back down the stairs with a hot pink backpack. Clothes and a stuffed bear are hanging out as he attempts to zip it shut.

"Put a jacket on her and take her to the clubhouse. I'll be there when I can."

Christ on a cracker. I scrub a hand through my dark hair, and he hands me the backpack. "I'm no damn babysitter. I've got plans. It's Friday night."

"Don't give a fuck what you have planned. Make sure she gets her meds and get her something to eat. I'm counting on you."

"Who is this kid?"

"I'll explain later. Just fucking do what you're told, East."

"Fine." I accept the backpack and take the medicine back out of the fridge and shove it in the side pocket.

Murder looks at Wylla Mae. "Listen, Cupcake. My brother here is gonna take you for a ride on his motorcycle. His name is East. You be a good girl and I'll bring you some ice cream later once I get your mom to see the doctor. Okay?" He pats her head and she nods as a tear trickles down her cheek.

Shit. *Double shit.* I know nothing good will come of this. I don't know who this kid is, but I can't go against my Prez. He better not have me in some shit with a custody issue or some shit. Last thing I need is to be called in for kidnapping this little girl.

Murder stomps back up the stairs. Halfway up he turns back to me. "Get her out of here now," he growls.

I shoot him a chin lift.

"All right, Lil' Lady. You got a jacket somewhere?"

She goes to the closet by the front door and tugs out a winter coat. It's black and has a gold princess crown embroidered with her name. She gets her coat on and puts some black furry boots on. Maybe her mom fell on hard times because her clothes are in good shape and name brand. I shouldn't judge so harshly but the empty fridge and dirty dishes pisses me off.

"You have anything else you need?"

"No," she whispers and coughs.

"Zip that jacket up."

She struggles and I end up placing the backpack on the couch and dropping to my knees to do it for her. The tip of her nose is red and crusted with dried snot. I want to wipe her face off, but I can hear Murder upstairs and know he'll have my ass if I don't get her out of here. "There. Let's go." I hand her the backpack and she loops her fingers around the straps dragging it behind her.

Outside, I shove the straps of the backpack over her shoulders. Lifting her up I plop her down on the seat of my bike. "Listen, I'll drive slow. You don't need to be scared. My helmet is too big for you, so you'll ride without one. Keep your feet on these pegs." I tap her leg and point. She nods. "When I get on, put your arms around my waist, head on my back. Don't lean or move. Don't panic. I'll keep you safe."

I get on and she curls her fingers in the belt loops of my jeans holding on tight. The sound of my Harley roars into the night.

The moment I roll up to the Devil's Playground, our clubhouse, I know bringing the kid here is a bad idea. A party is in full swing. I shut off my bike and once she lets go of my pants swing my leg over. I ruffle my fingers through her pale hair. "See nothing to it. You're a natural." I grip her waist and pluck her off the seat, planting her feet on the ground. "Keep your head down and stick to my side. Don't look at what's happening inside just keep walking until I tell you it's okay."

I trudge toward the entrance, the music growing louder. Fuck. This is no place for an angel.

No place at all. Fucking Murder. What the hell was he thinking tasking me with brat duty? This is some shit one of his muffler bunnies should be handling. What the hell am I supposed to do with her?

Here we fucking go. I push the door open, loud rock filtering through and blasting me right in the damn face along with a cloud of smoke. I scan the room and the festivities haven't started. I check my watch. The night is still young.

"Hey handsome," Mariah purrs, licking her lips and rubbing up on my right side, her fake tits spilling out of her neon green tube top. I'm in no mood for her and the bullshit she brings with her. Woman is nothing but pure drama. Catty and clingy as hell. Two things I don't want or need.

I push her off. "Not now."

"Shit." She notices my shadow. "Didn't know you had a kid, East."

"I don't."

"Wait you aren't into some sick shit, are you?"

My brow furrows and I ball my fist. "Fuck you for even saying some shit like that, you fuckin' dumb cunt." I shove past her and go to the bar and stick Wylla Mae on a stool. "Get her a Sprite," I yell over the noise to Slater.

He gives me a chin lift, grabs a can from the cooler, and slides it down the bar. I pop the tab. "Don't drink nothing or eat a damn thing unless I give it to you directly. No one here would hurt you but shit happens, and I'd rather be safe than sorry. Understood?"

Her doe eyes gaze up at me. She doesn't say anything but takes the pop and chugs.

"You hungry?"

"Uh huh."

"Come on. Let's see what we can find in the kitchen." She slides down the stool and curls into my side where I keep her pressed until we get there. It's only a matter of time before shit starts to get wild around here. The kitchen door swings open and Pam stands on the other side.

"What are you up to?" She raises her arms over her head, securing her dark curly hair in a ponytail.

"This is Wylla Mae, my charge for the evening. Whatchu' got good, fast, and hot?"

"I'd tell you but it's not appropriate for small ears." Her laughter rings out.

I shake my head. I walked straight into that one.

"Stick this in the fridge will ya." I dig the medicine out and toss the bottle her way.

"Aw, sweetie, are you sick?"

Wylla Mae sniffles and wipes at her nose reminding me that I need to wash that face. While Pam gets the medicine in the fridge and questions the kid about what she wants to eat I grab some paper towels and wet them.

"C'mere, Lil' Lady." I grip the back of her head with one hand and use my other to clean her face. She scrunches her nose and squirms. "There.

Good as new." I turn toward Pam and toss the paper towels in the trash. "You busy tonight?"

Her finger wags in my face. "Oh no, you aren't putting your job off on me. It's Friday night."

"Come on. You know I don't know shit about taking care of a sick kid."

"I'm sure you'll figure it out. Feed her. Give her water and the pink stuff as directed." She smirks.

"I'll owe you one."

"Hmm. You'll owe me more than one."

"I wanna stay with you, East," Wylla Mae shouts and barrels into my side, surprising the fuck outta me.

"You heard the lady." Pam winks at her and slides a grilled cheese sandwich onto a paper plate. "See you later, daddy." She cackles going out the door, leaving me on my own with Wylla Mae.

I cap the back of my neck and look down at Wylla Mae. "How old are you anyway, kid?"

"Eight and a half."

"Christ. You look six."

"Do not," she sasses then wheezes out a cough and kicks me in the shin.

"Ow shit. What'd you do that for?"

"Momma says you shouldn't say bad words. Now you owe me a quarter."

"I didn't. Never mind. You don't go around kicking people. Get your food," I growl at her.

Her bottom lip trembles but she doesn't shed any tears. Those doe eyes hold me captive, and I feel like a jerk. Wylla Mae is sick and with strangers. Who knows what happened with her mom or when Murder will come to collect her? I can see it in her gaze. Fear. Sadness. But there is something else there. A glimmer of hope. My heart constricts in my chest.

"I'm sorry I yelled at you, but you don't kick me."

"Okay."

"All right. I'm gonna take you upstairs to a room where you can watch Tv or whatever."

"Okay." Her hand shakes as she grabs the paper plate.

"Christ. Let me have it." I take it from her before she drops it, and she grabs my free hand wrapping her clammy fingers around mine, squeezing tight.

**

Upstairs, I pace the small room. I crash here sometimes when I've had too much to drink or simply don't want to make the ride home. It's not much but serves me when I need to scratch an itch or pass out. The space fits a full-sized bed, couch, small table, and a flat screen mounted on the wall over the dresser. Like I said it isn't much.

Wylla Mae is sprawled out on my bed hugging her teddy bear. I turn on some channel that only shows classic cartoons. She seems content and hasn't even bothered to ask about her mother once.

Not that I would have an answer for her. Hell, I don't even know who her mom is.

"Hey." I grab the remote control and press the button to turn the volume down on her show. "What's your mom's name?"

"Alexa."

"You got a dad?" Her head moves side to side. "An aunt, uncle, cousin, grandma?" There's gotta be someone else who can take her in until whatever is going on with her mom is settled.

"Just my mom."

Great. Of course. "Okay." I increase the volume on the Tv. I need a damn smoke. My head feels split in two. I go over to the window and crack it then dig through the top drawer of the dresser for my emergency cigarettes stash. Bingo. At least one thing has gone my way tonight. Back at the window I light up my Marlboro and take a hard drag. Tobacco pulls through my lungs in a familiar burn that I've grown addicted to feeling.

164

"You shouldn't be smoking in here." Wylla Mae glares at me up on her knees in the center of the bed, lips jutted out and a hand on her hip. She looks ready to pop off like a little firecracker. Little sassy assed brat is what she is. She looks like an angel till she opens that mouth. Kid was shy at first but now she won't shut the hell up.

"Why is that?"

"Because it's bad for you. You could get cancer and die or worse."

"What's worse than death?"

"You're exposing me to secondhand smoke and I'm just a kid."

I chuckle, blowing my smoke out the window.

"Why are you laughing?"

"I'm not."

"Are too," she sasses.

God this kid and her mouth. I pity the poor soul who marries her one day.

About Glenna

Glenna Maynard is a USA TODAY & Wall Street
Journal Bestselling Author most known for her
gritty Black Rebel Riders' MC saga.

She has a passion for writing antiheroes but
occasionally takes a walk on the sweeter side.
Bikers, Rockstars, the boy next door, Glenna writes
them all.

When she isn't arguing with the voices in her head
or drinking reader tears, she enjoys watching classic
TV shows with her two children and longtime
leading man. Her favorite books to read change
with her mood, but she always enjoys a good
historical romance.

Visit https://www.glennamaynard.com for more
information.

Available Now

<u>Black Rebel Riders' MC</u>

Grim The Beginning

Rumor

Baby

Striker

Romeo

Heart of A Rebel

A Rebel Love

A Rebel In The Roses

Blood of A Rebel

The Devil's Rebel

<u>Devils Rejects MC</u>

Hades' Flame

Boogeyman's Dream

Reaper's Till Death

Cupid's Arrow

Uno's Truth

Cocky's Fight

Black Rebel Devils MC

Moonshine & Mistletoe

Guns & Roses

Sex & Cigarettes

BRRMC Roadhouse Tales

Devil Dick

Pecker Wrecker

Cock Blocker

Sassy Pants

Sons Of Destruction

Dark Paradise: The Apocalypse

The Cruel Love Series

Cruel Love Book 1

Cruel Love Book 2

Royal Bastards MC

The Biker's Kiss

Lady & The Biker

Tempting The Biker

Keeping The Biker

The Biker's Lucky Charm

Taken By The Biker

Stand Alone Titles

Fabricated Christmas

Beauty & The Biker

Snow White & The Biker

Born Sinner

Lil' Red & The Big Bad Biker

Making Her Mine

Dirty Love

Dirty Truth

Don't Let Me Go

Jameson's Addiction

My Best Friend's Girl

Calder & Maggie

Falling For The Bad Boy

Tucker

<u>Cowritten with Dawn Martens</u>

You Wreck Me (Prospects)

You Break Me (Prospects)

You Kill Me (Prospects)

You Belong To Me (Prospects)

Sacking The Player